James Monroe

by

Stuart A. Kallen

Visit us at
www.abdopub.com

Published by ABDO Publishing Company, 4940 Viking Drive, Edina, MN 55435.

Printed in the United States.

Graphic Design: John Hamilton
Cover Design: MacLean Tuminelly
Cover photo: Corbis
Interior photos and illustrations:
Art Commision of the City of New York, p. 32
Corbis, p. 5, 6, 7, 9, 11, 15, 16, 17, 19, 21, 23, 24, 25, 27, 29, 31, 33, 35, 43, 51, 55, 57, 59
John Hamilton, p. 26, 44
Library of Congress, p. 13
North Wind Pictures, p. 37, 47, 49
White House Historical Association, p. 39, 41

Library of Congress Cataloging-in-Publication Data
Kallen, Stuart A., 1955-
James Monroe / Stuart A. Kallen.
p. cm. — (The founding fathers)
Includes index.
Summary: Discusses the early life, career, family, and contributions of the fifth president of the United States.
ISBN 1-57765-230-4
1. Monroe, James, 1758-1831—Juvenile literature. 2. Presidents—United States—Biography—Juvenile literature. [1. Monroe, James, 1758-1831 2. Presidents.] I. Title.

E372.K35 2001
973.5'4'092—dc21
[B]

98-013304

Contents

Introduction

IT WAS CHRISTMAS DAY, 1776. The Revolutionary War was going badly for the American soldiers. British troops had driven the Americans out of New York City, across New Jersey, and into Pennsylvania. The British had hired German soldiers, called Hessians, to fight with them.

While the Hessians ate, drank, and played cards on Christmas Day, American soldiers were standing in freezing rain on the shores of the Delaware River. The rain turned to snow and back into rain again. As night fell, the 2,500 American soldiers prepared to march. But first they had to cross the river.

Facing page: A portrait of President James Monroe, fifth president of the United States, by James Herring.

George Washington stands tall as his boat crosses the turbulent water of the Delaware River.

Hour after hour the men poled their boats 300 yards (274 meters) across the Delaware. Lieutenant James Monroe stood guard in the dark. When a farmer told Monroe to get off his land, the soldier refused. The farmer thought Monroe was British. When he found out Monroe was an American, the farmer brought him food and warm tea.

After 10 hours crossing rough, icy waters, the army was ready to march nine miles (14 km) into Trenton, where the Hessians slept. As the column slipped and stumbled through the dark, General George Washington urged them to press on.

By dawn the tired army surrounded the village of Trenton. The Hessians were sleeping off their late-night Christmas Eve celebrations. Washington's plan had caught them by surprise. The Hessians panicked and fired their muskets wildly. A few Hessians tried to turn a cannon around in a narrow street. James Monroe and another man led an attack on them. Bullets were flying everywhere. Suddenly, Monroe was thrown onto his back. A musket bullet had ripped into his shoulder. As Washington's troops put the Hessians on the run, 17-year-old Lt. Monroe lay bleeding in the street.

General Washington's early morning surprise attack on the Hessian soldiers at Trenton proved successful. Future president James Monroe was wounded in the battle.

JAMES MONROE WAS BORN IN Westmoreland County, Virginia, on April 28, 1758. The Monroes were a typical middle-class family of eighteenth-century Virginia. They owned large tracts of land and used slaves to work their tobacco fields.

Spence Monroe, James's father, was also a carpenter. Since there were few skilled carpenters in the colonies, Spence was in great demand.

Like all sons of Virginia farmers, James learned to ride a horse and hunt. Even as a boy, he was a skilled marksman and rider. Unlike most children of the time, James went to school. His favorite subjects were Latin and math.

During this era, the Virginia colony was a merry place to live. People in Virginia made almost everything they needed. But some things had to be imported. Spices, fine furniture, paint, mirrors, clocks, and musical instruments were shipped in from England or France. And people especially liked clothes and fashions from England.

A worker harvests tobacco by hand.

Paying for a War

WHEN JAMES WAS BORN, England was fighting a war against France. The war began as the two countries argued over who would control forts and trading posts in America's western territories. Because Native Americans were helping the French, the conflict was called the French and Indian War. The British king, King George III, ruled the American colonies. But England was also busy fighting the French in Europe. American people in the colonies were pretty much left to rule themselves.

The British won the war against France in 1763. But they were left with huge debts. The British thought Americans would be glad to pay taxes to help cover the costs of the war. After all, the war had driven France out of America.

England's King George III.

The British government, called Parliament, passed the Stamp Act in 1765. It put taxes on newspapers, legal papers, playing cards, and other printed matter. Americans were outraged. After a year of protests—some of them violent—Parliament repealed the Stamp Act.

The Boston Tea Party

IN 1767, PARLIAMENT PASSED another tax law, called the Townsend Act. The Townsend Act put taxes on lead, glass, paint, paper, and tea. In protest, Americans boycotted, or refused to buy, these items. By the time James Monroe was 15 years old, tensions between America and Britain had reached new heights.

In 1773, a group of men disguised themselves as Mohawk Indians. In protest to the tea tax, the men dumped 342 cases of British tea in Boston Harbor. The Boston Tea Party enraged King George III. The British government closed Boston Harbor, stating that the busy port would remain completely shut down until the tea was paid for. Soon colonists in Massachusetts ran low on food. Business came to a standstill. In Virginia, the tensions caused tobacco prices to drop sharply. Many Virginia farmers went deeply into debt.

American colonists, some in disguise as Mohawk Indians, dump British tea into Boston Harbor.

Student to Soldier

IN THIS TENSE POLITICAL climate, James Monroe headed off to college. It was 1774 and he was 16 years old. Monroe went to William and Mary College in Williamsburg, the capital of colonial Virginia.

While Monroe was studying hard at college, America was preparing for war. Thousands of British soldiers were camped out on Boston Common, a park in the center of town. The British soldiers were called "redcoats" and "lobster backs" because of their uniforms. Meanwhile, American solders were training to fight the British. The Americans were called minutemen because they were prepared to fight at a minute's notice.

Facing page: A statue at the Old North Bridge in Concord, Massachusetts, commemorates the minutemen who stood against the British during the Revolutionary War.

The Revolution Begins

ON APRIL 19, 1775, the redcoats marched into Lexington, Massachusetts, to seize gunpowder that belonged to the minutemen. Led by General Thomas Gage, governor of Massachusetts and commander of all British soldiers in North America, a battle began between the patriots and the British. Eight Americans were shot and killed. The American Revolution had begun.

James Monroe was still a teenager attending William and Mary College in Virginia when fighting broke out between Britain and the colonies.

American colonists and British soldiers exchange fire at the Battle of Lexington, the first skirmish in the United State War of Independence.

News of the battle of Lexington reached Williamsburg nine days later. It was Monroe's seventeenth birthday. The students formed militias to fight the British. Monroe quickly signed up.

Monroe was eager to fight the British. He quit school and left for New York with a company of other young men. When they got to New York City, the militiamen joined General George Washington's Continental Army.

Meanwhile, in Philadelphia, Thomas Jefferson wrote the Declaration of Independence. The Declaration of Independence was approved by the Continental Congress on July 4, 1776. The document told Britain that America was an independent nation.

Facing page: A copy of the United States Declaration of Independence.

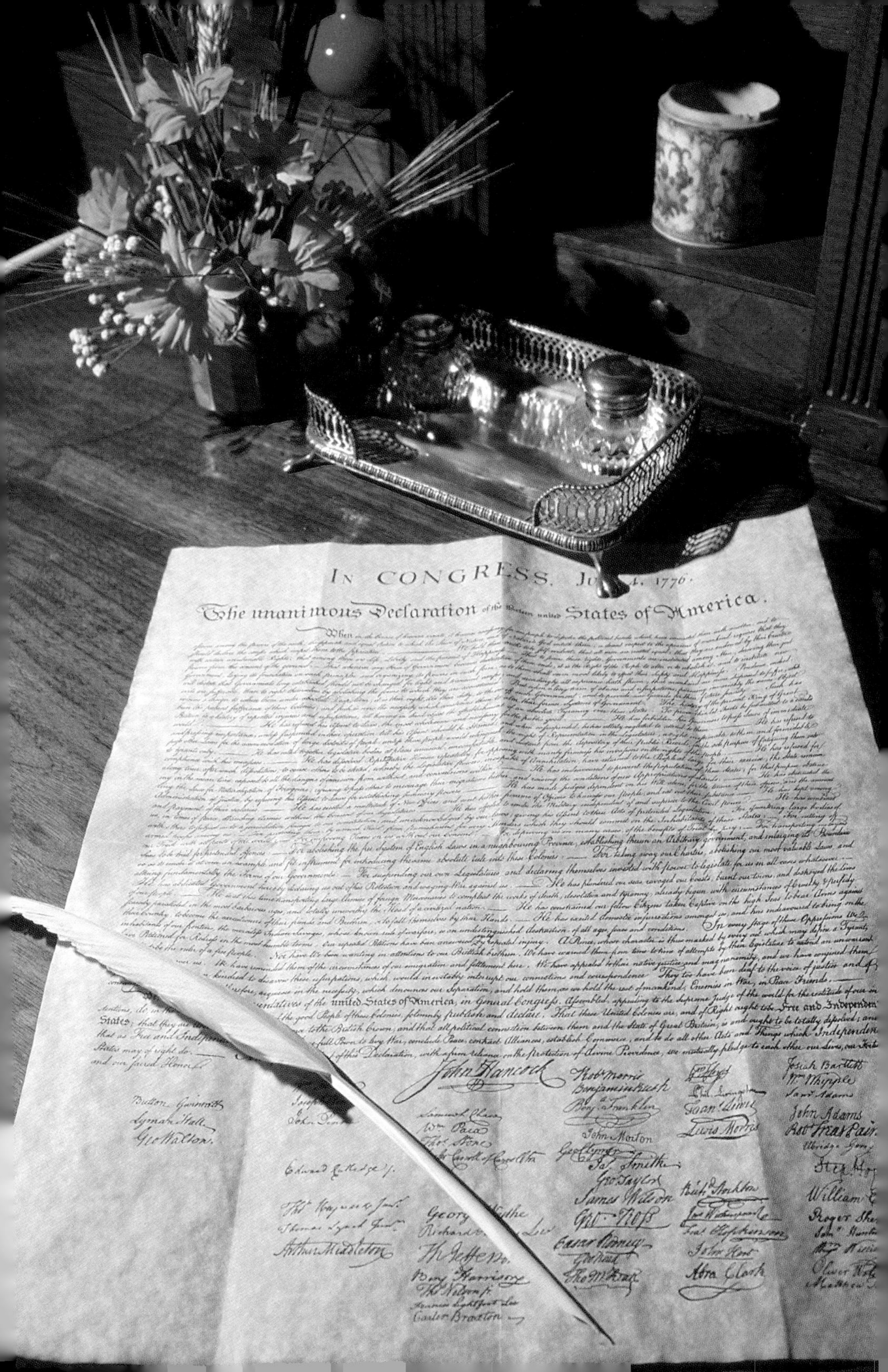
IN CONGRESS,
The unanimous Declaration
States of America.
John Hancock

Battling the British

MONROE SAW HIS first battles in the fall of 1776. The Americans fought the British in New York's Harlem Heights (now Central Park). They also fought in White Plains, New York. The Americans were brave. But they lacked decent supplies and were poorly trained.

The British pushed the Americans out of New York City. The Continental Army retreated across New Jersey throughout November. By December, they finally were pushed across the Delaware River into Pennsylvania. During this time, Monroe served as a scout, watching the movements of British troops.

Facing page: An actor portrays an American scout.

No Support on the Home Front

AMERICAN SOLDIERS were a rag-tag bunch. They didn't have uniforms or warm coats. Some were frontier riflemen who were good shots. But they didn't know how to follow military orders. To make matters worse, the troops had little support from the colonists. Most Americans didn't support the British. But they didn't want to risk being arrested for treason by English troops.

George Washington needed a big victory. He wanted to convince Americans to support the revolution and support his battered army. Washington had a plan. The British had signed up Hessian (German) soldiers to help them. On Christmas Day, the Hessians were celebrating in Trenton, New Jersey. They were drinking, eating, singing, and playing cards. Washington knew that after the Germans drank all night, they would be in no shape to fight in the morning.

American soldiers were often poorly clothed and outfitted. These fife and drum players are from A.M. Willard's famous painting.

Washington's Daring Plan

ON A SNOWY CHRISTMAS night, 2,500 American soldiers gathered at McConkey's Ferry on the Delaware River. They climbed into dozens of boats, battling the stiff wind that beat into their faces. Officer John Fitzgerald later wrote, "It is fearfully cold and raw. A terrible night for the soldiers [some] who have no shoes...but I have not heard one man complain." James Monroe stood guard as the boats crossed the river.

General George Washington, by artist Rembrandt Peale.

An annual historical reenactment commemorates George Washington's crossing of the Delaware River in 1776 to surprise Hessian troops in Trenton.

After 10 hours on the water, the army was ready to march the nine miles (14.5 km) into Trenton, where they knew the Hessians slept. The long column of soldiers slipped and stumbled through the dark snowy night.

When the Americans reached Trenton, the Germans were asleep in their beds. The Hessians were completely surprised when the Americans arrived. Some tried to fight back, but they were quickly overrun. In the fighting, Monroe took a bullet in the shoulder and was seriously wounded. Luckily, a doctor was there to save the young lieutenant's life.

In less than two hours 900 German soldiers surrendered to the Americans. The victory raised the spirits of Washington's small army. For his bravery, Monroe was promoted to captain.

A close-up view of a musket firing.

Hessian soldiers, captured in the Battle of Trenton, being taken to Philadelphia with General George Washington and his troops.

Winter at Valley Forge

MONROE HAD healed enough to rejoin the army in the summer of 1777. He was appointed as an aide to General William Alexander. After the Battle of Brandywine in September, Monroe was promoted to major. But the British continued to pound the Americans. By the winter of 1777, the British had taken over Philadelphia.

The British settled into Philadelphia for the winter. They had plenty of food, drink, and warm quarters. The Americans retreated to a hilly camp called Valley Forge, 18 miles (29 km) northwest of Philadelphia.

The Continental soldiers built crude huts from twigs and mud. In a few weeks, thousands of these drafty huts covered the hills. Twelve men packed every cabin, where they huddled around smoky fires. Icy winds blew through the walls. In December the meat ran out. Men made pasty cakes of flour and water and baked them over hot stones.

If food was bad, clothing was even worse. Dr. Albigence Waldo wrote of a typical soldier's clothes. "His bare feet are seen through his worn-out shoes, his legs nearly naked from the tattered remains of an only pair of stockings, his breeches not sufficient to cover his nakedness, his shirt hanging in strings." Before the cruel winter ended, 2,500 patriots lay dead.

George Washington meets with aide Marquis Lafayette at Valley Forge, where the Continental Army suffered through the cold winter of 1777-78 during the American Revolution.

"A Thousand Hats Tossed in the Air"

MONROE WAS LUCKY enough to spend the winter in Reading, Pennsylvania, with General William Alexander. The officers there had better food and shelter. In spring, the soldiers were told that France had come to help them with training, soldiers, and money. Washington wrote that when he told his troops the news, "there were a thousand hats tossed in the air."

In June, Monroe led a scouting party out of Valley Forge. On the eve of the Battle of Monmouth, in New Jersey, Monroe captured three redcoats. Then he sent a note to Washington to tell him where the British were camped.

Molly Pitcher helping load cannon at the Battle of Monmouth in New Jersey. The battle was a major victory for the Americans.

Monroe was ready to become a military leader. He went back to Virginia with a letter from Washington. The general had said that Monroe was a brave, active, and sensible officer. But Monroe could not find soldiers to lead in Virginia. While he waited, Monroe studied law. He also became an aide to Thomas Jefferson, who had been elected governor of Virginia.

The Revolution is Won

IN 1780, THE BRITISH attacked Virginia. Thousands of Virginians rushed to join the military. Monroe finally had his soldiers. He was appointed colonel of a regiment.

In 1781, the British attacked Yorktown, Virginia. With the help of French troops, the redcoats were defeated. The Virginians celebrated at a dance in a Fredericksburg tavern. George Washington was there. So was James Monroe. At the age of 23, Monroe was a veteran of many battles. He had proven his bravery time and time again. Now he could celebrate the fact that he had helped America become a free country.

A portrait of James Monroe, war hero.

American troops capture a British stronghold during the Battle of Yorktown.

The Virginia Politician

LIKE MANY SOLDIERS returning to everyday life, Monroe was restless. His father had died and left him the large family farm. But Monroe did not want to be a farmer. He sold the land.

Monroe didn't want an army career. He decided instead to continue his law studies in France or England. But before he left, he was asked to serve in the Virginia General Assembly.

Monroe's public service began in 1782. At the age of 24, he was one of the youngest members of the assembly. But Monroe was a serious young man who was serious about the business of government. At the assembly, he met another young man who felt the way he did. James Madison was just leaving the assembly as Monroe was joining it. The two became immediate friends.

Facing page: a portrait of James Monroe by painter Alonzo Chappel.

Traveling the Territories

IN 1783, MONROE represented Virginia at the Fourth Continental Congress. Many of the delegates he met there had signed the Declaration of Independence in the Second Continental Congress. The Fourth Congress was meeting to sign a peace treaty with Britain, officially ending the Revolutionary War. When Monroe arrived he was pleased to see Thomas Jefferson.

The Fourth Congress had many problems to solve. How would new states be admitted into the United States? How should the western lands be divided into states? Jefferson simply wanted to draw out states on a map, making each one about the same size. Monroe didn't agree.

When the congress was in recess, Monroe decided to see the western territories for himself. Travel in the frontier was dangerous and tiring. He wrote to Jefferson: "It is possible that I may lose my scalp from the temper of the Indians but if either a little fighting or a great deal of running will save it, I shall escape safe." Later three men in Monroe's party were killed by Indians—Monroe escaped.

Monroe was impressed with America's western lands. He told Jefferson the rivers, lakes, and mountains should be each state's boundaries.

Monroe continued to serve in the Continental Congress. But he became discouraged. The states fought among themselves. No one cared for the common good. And the country was poor. Salaries of congressmen were low. Monroe decided to return to his law practice.

A mail stage makes its way through the western territories in the early 1800s.

Settling Down

MONROE SETTLED in Fredericksburg, Virginia. He brought with him his new wife, Elizabeth Kortright, whom he had married in New York City. Kortright was a tall, beautiful woman whose family was wealthy and well known in New York society. New Yorkers were shocked when she married Monroe—an "unknown" congressman from the South. James and Elizabeth had a daughter in July 1787.

James did well in Fredericksburg. But he longed to be back in public office. Meanwhile, delegates from the 13 colonies met in Philadelphia to hammer out a new government. The Constitutional Convention spent a long hot summer writing the United States Constitution. On September 17, 1787, the convention approved the Constitution.

To his disappointment, Monroe was not asked to serve at the Constitutional Convention. But he was asked to be on the Virginia Ratifying Committee. That group would vote to ratify (approve) the Constitution.

When Monroe read the document, he was upset. The Constitution said nothing about the rights of common citizens. Monroe voted against ratifying the Constitution. The Constitution was approved anyway. Later, the Bill of Rights was added to spell out the freedoms for which the American Revolution had been fought.

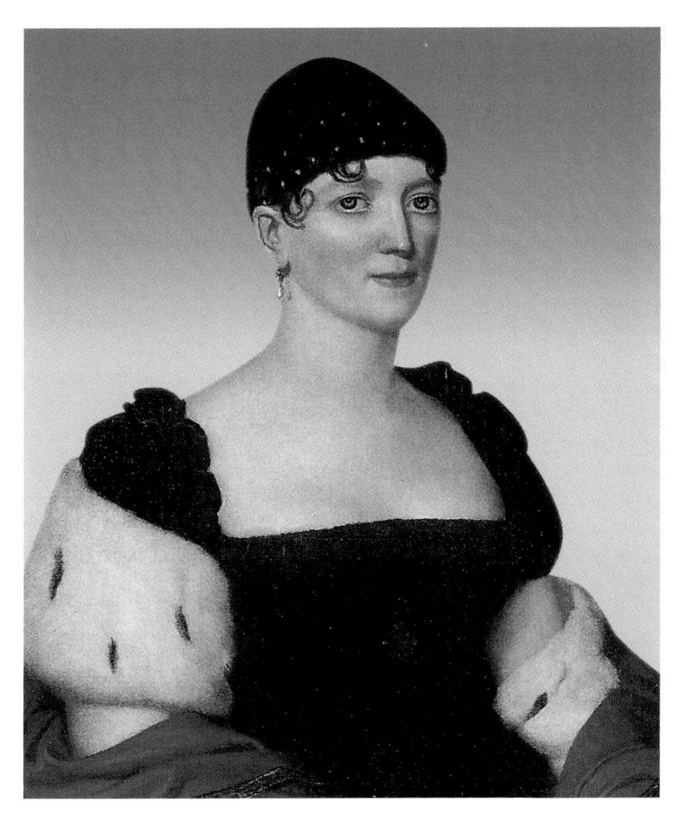

A portrait of Elizabeth Monroe.

Senator Monroe

IN 1790, MONROE RAN for the United States Senate and won. The main issue concerning America was in far-away France. France had helped America win independence from England. In 1789, French people wanted changes made in their own country's government, and the French Revolution began. There was massive bloodshed in the streets of Paris. (Revolutionaries eventually even chopped off the head of their king, King Louis XVI, in 1793.)

Some Americans supported the French. Like Monroe, they believed that the government should be run by common citizens, farmers, and anyone else who could do the job. These people, mostly southerners, called themselves Republicans.

Some, like George Washington, felt that government should be run by bankers, lawyers, and businessmen. These men, most of them from

James Monroe won election to the United States Senate in 1790.

northern states, called themselves Federalists. Many Federalists were engaged in trade with England.

When France declared war on England in 1793, the Republicans and the Federalists were deeply divided over the issue. By that time most Americans were horrified by the bloodshed of the French Revolution. The United States was still an ally of France. The French expected help in their war against England.

The Foreign Minister

PRESIDENT WASHINGTON sent James Monroe to France as the U.S. Minister. But Washington did not want to help France fight England. In the meantime, Washington sent John Jay to England. Jay was to sign a treaty that would improve relations between the United States and Britain. When the French found out about the Jay Treaty, they were furious. Washington recalled Monroe from France and the senator returned home bitterly disappointed.

Back home in Virginia, Monroe was a well-known hero. He was elected governor in 1799. Things seemed to be going well until a personal tragedy struck. James and Elizabeth's baby son died in September 1800. Monroe, however, went on to complete his term in office, improving schools, building roads, and deepening channels dredged in the Potomac and James Rivers.

While Monroe was governor of Virginia, his friend Thomas Jefferson was elected president. In 1803, Jefferson asked Monroe to return to France for a very important mission. Spain had just given the Louisiana Territory to France. The French, who were still mad at America, had closed the French port of New Orleans to American ships. But France desperately needed money to fight Britain. Jefferson wanted Monroe to buy New Orleans from the French emperor, Napoleon Bonaparte.

Within a few weeks of his arrival, Monroe had purchased the entire Louisiana Territory for $15 million. It was an incredible purchase. Overnight the United States doubled in size.

The ceremony of land transfer for the Louisiana Purchase in 1804. United States Commissioner Captain Amos Stoddard takes a document from Lansat, Napoleon's representative.

The Louisiana Territory, bought from France for only $15 million, doubled the size of the United States.

Meanwhile, British ships were stopping American ships, taking American sailors, and forcing them to serve in the British navy. Jefferson sent Monroe to England to put a stop to this. But the British treated him rudely. After getting nowhere, Monroe was off to Spain.

Spain had agreed to give Florida to France in 1800. The United States thought Florida was part of the Louisiana Purchase. But in 1805, Spain still controlled Florida and wouldn't even talk to Monroe.

Relations with the British continued to get worse. The British announced that they would capture any American ship carrying war goods to France. This meant that every American ship had to stop in England to be searched for war goods. The French said they would seize any ship that obeyed the British rule. American trade with Europe was in shambles. Monroe returned to America. "We have no friends anywhere," he wrote.

Back in Virginia, Monroe was once again elected governor. In 1808, his old friend James Madison was elected president.

The War of 1812

MADISON ASKED MONROE TO be secretary of state in 1811. It was not an easy job. France and Britain continued to fight. Both countries seized American ships and sailors. The ships were looted and burned. The American sailors were forced to fight under harsh discipline in the British navy. Jefferson summed up American feelings when he said: "As for France and England, the one is a den of robbers, the other of pirates."

Soon British warships were right outside New York Harbor. They swooped down on American ships the minute they sailed out into the Atlantic Ocean. This was too much for Americans. On June 18, 1812, America declared war on England.

The War of 1812 did not have to happen. Two days before America declared war, England said it would stop kidnapping American sailors. But in

British sailors kidnapping Americans to serve in the British Navy.

those days it took weeks for the news to travel across the ocean. By the time Americans heard about England's offer of peace, it was too late. America soldiers had already lost several bloody battles in Canada. Monroe and others would not quit the fight. Later, most Americans regretted this decision.

The British did not want another costly war. But they fought on. By 1814, the war was going very badly for the Americans. They had been losing battles steadily for two years. In August, the British invaded Maryland. Soon British soldiers began marching to Washington, D.C. Advisors to President Madison did not believe the British would attack the city. But on August 18, Monroe warned the president to remove important government files. Then Monroe set out on horseback to scout the British advance, much like he had done in 1776.

Washington Burns

THE AMERICAN ARMY was poorly organized and melted away in front of British fire. On August 24, the British marched into Washington, D.C. without firing a shot. They entered the White House and found a table set for lunch. They ate the meal that Dolley Madison had prepared for her husband, the president. Afterward they made a large pile of White House furniture and set the building ablaze. While the White House burned the British torched the Capitol, the Navy Yard, and the bridge across the Potomac.

On August 25, a large rainstorm put out the fires. The British troops left for Baltimore.

When Madison returned to his destroyed home, he was enraged. He fired the secretary of war and appointed James Monroe to the job. As secretary of state, Monroe had tried to get Britain to end the war. As secretary of war, he directed the troops to fight. Finally, on Christmas Eve, 1814, the Americans and the British negotiated an end to the War of 1812.

British troops burning and looting the lightly defended Washington, D.C.

President Monroe

AFTER THE WAR, everyone expected Monroe to become president. He did not disappoint the nation. In 1816, he was elected as the fifth president of the United States. After his inauguration, Monroe went on a three-month tour of the United States.

Monroe traveled by horse, carriage, steamboat, and at times by foot. He went as far west as Detroit. He went as far north as Portland, Maine. Later he went down south. Everywhere Monroe went, crowds lined the streets. There were bands playing, guns saluting, and parties. One newspaper proclaimed that it was "The Era of Good Feeling." The phrase stuck. For many years after, Monroe's terms were called the "Era of Good Feeling."

Americans were impressed with their president. But Monroe seemed stuck in the 1700s. He still dressed in velvet knee breeches and silk

James Monroe's inauguration as the fifth United States president. The ruins of Washington, D.C., can be seen in the background.

stockings. Other men wore trousers. Monroe still wore his hair long, powdered, and tied back with a ribbon. Most men cut their hair short. But Monroe's old-fashioned appearance proudly reminded people of the American Revolution.

By 1817, Monroe was back in the White House. While he had been touring the country, workmen were repairing damage done by the British.

The First Term

TWO BIG ISSUES marked Monroe's first term as president: The United States still wanted Florida. And there was a deep division between the North and South over the issue of slavery.

Florida was a problem because it was full of outlaws. Bandits would steal cattle in Georgia and escape to Florida, where U.S. marshals could not arrest them. In 1818, Monroe sent Andrew Jackson to Florida to restore order. Jackson was reckless. He attacked Spanish forts and killed many Spanish people. Finally in 1821, Monroe convinced Spain to give up Florida.

Now a larger problem loomed. Slavery had divided the country since before the Revolution. The Missouri Compromise of 1820-21 was an attempt to solve the disputes between free and slave states in the United States. In 1818,

Missouri Territory, where many settlers owned slaves, applied to join the Union. Bitter controversy ensued, because many northerners wished to limit the addition of new slave states.

An amendment was made to the Missouri statehood bill. It indicated that the state would gradually eliminate slavery. The amendment was defeated in the United States Senate, and Congress adjourned without passing the statehood bill.

In the next session of Congress, while the status of Missouri was still undecided, Alabama was admitted (1819) to the Union as a slave state. The free and slave states were now equally represented in the Senate.

The Speaker of the House pushed through a series of measures that came to be called the Missouri Compromise. Missouri *and* Maine were to be admitted as slave and free states. Monroe supported the Missouri Compromise because he did not want a civil war to break out. Other people believed he should have stood up against slavery. But he did not. It temporarily quieted the debate. But the Missouri Compromise did nothing to solve the dilemma of slavery in a society that believed in democracy.

The Second Term

JAMES MONROE TOOK the oath of office for a second time on March 5, 1821. He was 63 years old. No one ran against him, so he did not have trouble getting elected.

Monroe's second term is probably best remembered for the Monroe Doctrine. The doctrine stated that America would not become entangled in wars and politics of foreign countries. But it also stated the foreign powers could not meddle in North or South America.

This sounded simple. But European nations were ready to send their huge armies into South America. Monroe was afraid they would try to grab American land in the west. The Europeans bitterly disliked the Monroe Doctrine. How dare the United States, a poor country with no standing army, tell them what to do? In the end, no nations ever invaded South America. It is probably because England had made the same claim as

Monroe. But later presidents such as James Polk, Grover Cleveland, and Theodore Roosevelt used the Monroe Doctrine when facing foreign threats. For over 90 years, the United States never involved themselves in Europe's affairs, until World War I broke out in 1917.

A painting by Clyde De Land showing the birth of the Monroe Doctrine. (From left to right): John Irving Adams; William Harris Crawford; William Wirt; President James Monroe (standing); John Caldwell Calhoun; Daniel D. Tompkins; and John McLean.

The President Retires

JAMES MONROE LEFT office on March 4, 1825. John Quincy Adams was the new president. Monroe was tired of politics. He wrote: "I shall be heartily rejoiced when the term of my service expires and I may return home in peace with my family."

Retirement would have been pleasant. But his wife Elizabeth died in 1830. The ex-president never recovered from the loss. His health declined as he went to live with his daughter in New York City.

Four years earlier, Thomas Jefferson and John Adams had both died on the Fourth of July, 1826. Monroe too, died on July 4, in 1831. Huge crowds of people attended his funeral in New York City. Bells tolled and guns fired in salute all over town. Monroe was buried in New York. But in 1858, Virginia requested that the former president be re-buried in his home state. Monroe's remains were moved to Richmond, Virginia.

President James Monroe.

Conclusion

JAMES MONROE WAS the last president who had fought in the American Revolution. He watched his country change from a British colony to one of the largest countries in the world. He fought for his beliefs on the battlefield. And he fought with words in the courts and palaces of foreign countries. Above it all, he was brave, honest, and sincere. Maybe Jefferson put it best when he said: "Monroe was so honest that if you turned his soul inside out, there would not be a spot on it."

Facing page: A portrait of President James Monroe, by Gilbert Stuart.

Timeline

April 28, 1758	James Monroe born in Westmoreland County, Virginia.
1774	At age 16, goes to William and Mary College in Williamsburg, Virginia.
1775	Quits school and travels to New York City to join General George Washington's Continental Army.
1776	Wounded at Battle of Trenton.
1783	Represents Virginia at the Fourth Continental Congress.
1786	Marries Elizabeth Kortright.
1790	Becomes a United States Senator.
1794	Appointed Minister to France.
1799	Governor of Virginia.
1803	Purchases Louisiana Territory from France.
1811	Appointed Secretary of State.
1814	Appointed Secretary of War.
1816	Elected 5th President of the United States.
1820	Reelected - no one runs against him. Receives every electoral vote, except one.
1823	Monroe Doctrine stated in his 7th message to Congress.
July 4, 1831	Monroe dies in New York City at the age of 73.

PBS's "The American President" Series

http://www.americanpresident.org/KoTrain/Courses/JMO/JMO_In_Brief.htm

Internet Public Library: Presidents of the United States

http://www.ipl.org/ref/POTUS/jmonroe.html

The Presidents of the United States—The White House

http://www.whitehouse.gov/history/presidents/jm5.html

Grolier Presents: The American Presidency

http://gi.grolier.com/presidents/ea/bios/05pmonr.html

Monticello Avenue

http://avenue.org/ashlawn/docs/bio-monroe.htm

James Monroe Museum and Memorial Library

http://www.artcom.com/museums/vs/gl/22401-58.htm

Virtual Tour of Monroe's Home—Ash Lawn Highland

http://monticello.avenue.org/ashlawn/docs/tour-virtual.htm

American Revolution: the war between Great Britain and its American colonies that lasted from 1775 to 1783. America won its independence in the war.

Bill of Rights: a statement of the rights of the people that make up the first ten amendments to the United States Constitution. Some of the amendments guarantee free speech, protection from search and seizure, and the right of a militia to bear arms.

boycott: to try to change the actions of a company or government by refusing to buy their products.

The Colonies: the British territories that made up the first 13 states of the United States. The 13 colonies were the states of New Hampshire, Massachusetts, Rhode Island, Connecticut, New York, New Jersey, Pennsylvania, Delaware, Maryland, Virginia, North Carolina, South Carolina, and Georgia.

Constitution: the document that spells out the principles and laws that govern the United States.

Constitutional Convention: the meeting of men who wrote the United States Constitution.

Continental Army: the army that fought the British in the Revolutionary War.

Continental Congress: lawmakers who governed the 13 colonies after they declared their independence from Great Britain.

Declaration of Independence: the document written by Thomas Jefferson that declared America's independence from Great Britain.

Federalist: a political party that favors a strong central government over the states.

inauguration: a formal ceremony held to swear a person into office.

militia: a body of citizens enrolled in military service during a time of emergency.

ratify: to express approval of a document such as the United States Constitution.

treason: violation of loyalty to one's own country, especially by calling for the government's overthrow.

Index